Grama's
HUG

To Kathy—for not leaving without a hug.

Grama's
HUG

Amy Nielander

PAGE
STREET
KiDS

May loved to visit Grama
every summer and watch
the stars.

*"Let's say goodnight to
the stars, May."*

Books

Then one cold day,
May came to live with her.

"Are you ready, May?"

"More hugs please, Grama."

May and Grama had always been a team.
Now they were inseparable. When school started,
May wished it was Grama's first day, too.

"And here is the biggest hug
in the world . . . I love you, May."

"Love you, too."

May and Grama watched the birds together every day.

They sparkled in winter,

flickered in spring,

and soared in the summer.

May wondered if she and Grama
could soar just like them.

"Thank you for the mighty wings, May.
We will be the highest-flying
birds in the world!"

"I'm gliding over the treetops, May . . ."

"I'm flying over Earth, Grama!
Astronaut May reporting new planet ahead!"

More first days of school came and went.

"Time to fly off to first grade! I love you."

"Love you too, Grama. Takeoff in 3 . . . 2 . . . 1!"

May wanted to take off to the stars one day.

So, every year she prepared for the space fair
and Grama eagerly assisted.

"Grama, what's my time?"

3rd Grade SPACE FAIR

"10 seconds! A record speed!"

Best JET PACK

"Introducing . . . Concept 33."

4th Grade SPACE FAIR

"It's my favorite, Astronaut May!"

Best SPACE SUIT

"*Real astronauts don't have broken Space Pets, Grama.*"

"*Even real astronauts need a break, love.*"

Their hard work paid off.

"Wait! Wait!
What about our goodbye?"

Now May was heading to
space camp for a whole month.

*"I miss my little astronaut already.
I'll be thinking about you every day."*

"Love you, Grama!"

"Love you, too . . ."

While May was busy at camp,

Grama's days passed very, very,

very slowly. At last, May was due home . . .

and she brought exciting news!

SPACE CAMP
Exceptional
Cadet

Space
Times
10-year-old astronaut

May's first day as
an astronaut arrived.

"Are you ready?"

"Ready."

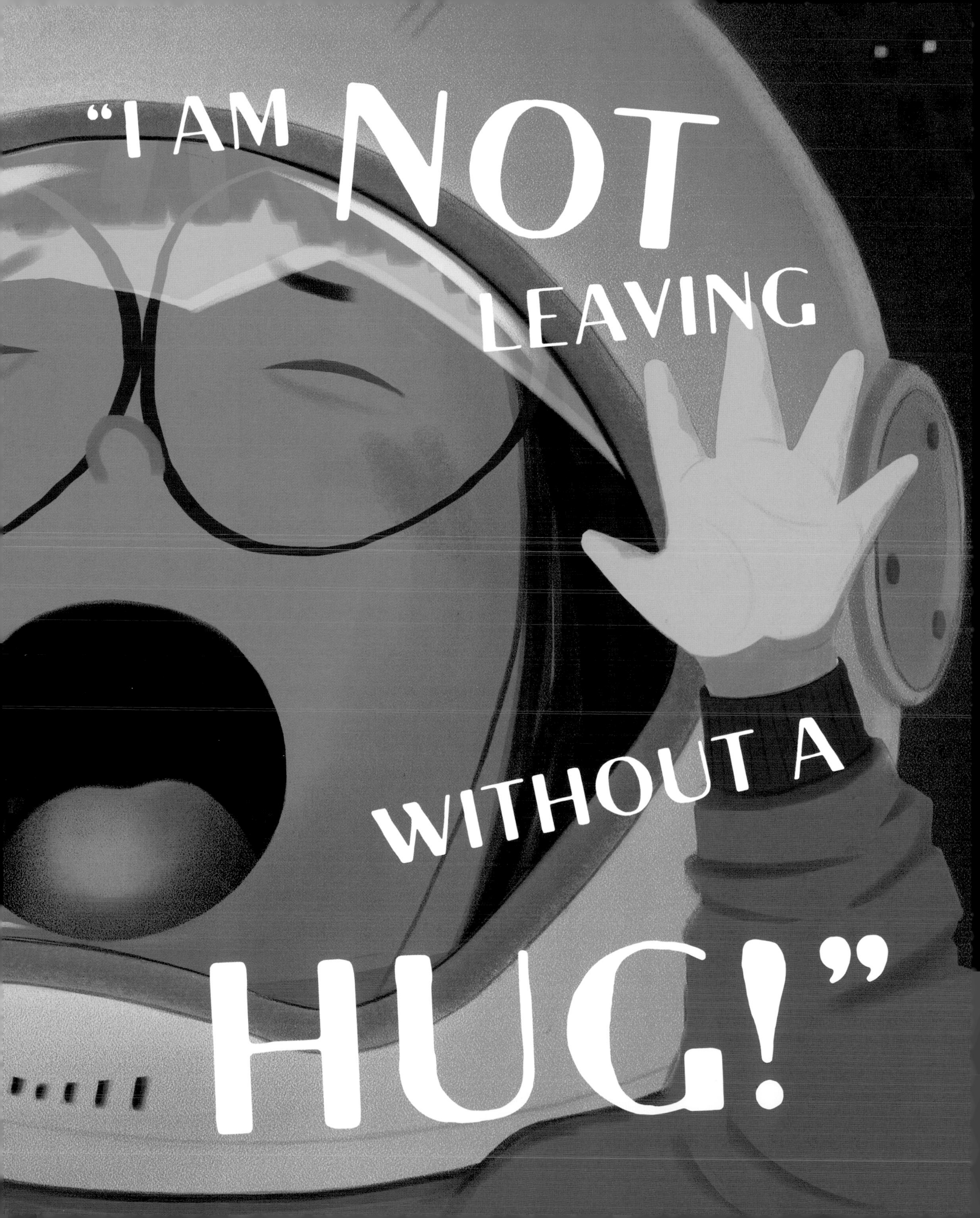

"I AM NOT LEAVING WITHOUT A HUG!"